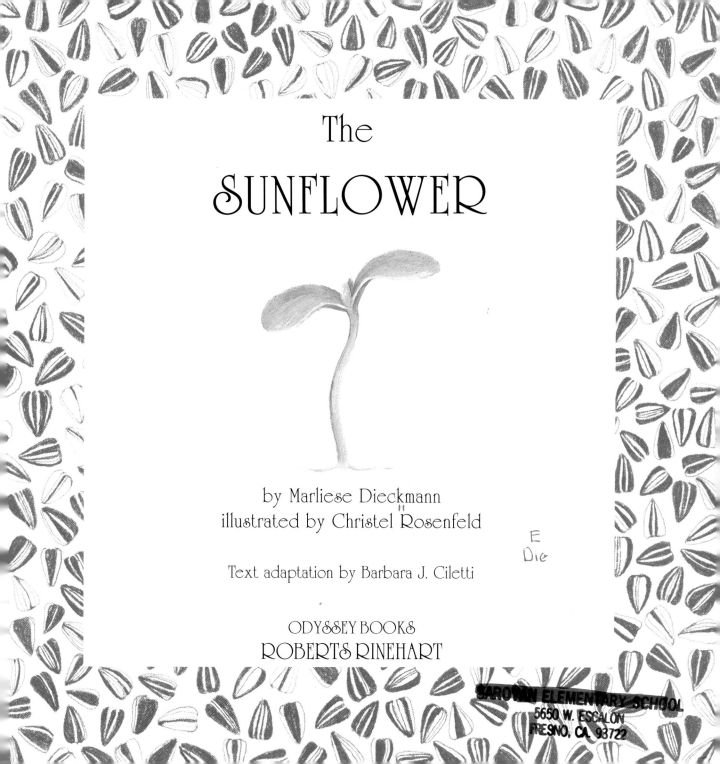

The
SUNFLOWER

by Marliese Dieckmann
illustrated by Christel Rosenfeld

Text adaptation by Barbara J. Ciletti

ODYSSEY BOOKS
ROBERTS RINEHART

First published in Germany under the Title Die Sonnenblume
© 1981 Verlag Heinrich Ellermann Munchen
English language text adaptation 1994 by Barbara J. Ciletti

Published in the United States of America by
Roberts Rinehart Publishers,
P.O. Box 666, Niwot, CO 80544
and
Barbara J. Ciletti
2421 Redwood Ct.
Longmont, CO 80503
Imprint: Odyssey Books

Published in the United Kingdom and Ireland by
Roberts Rinehart Publishers, Main Street, Schull
West Cork, Republic of Ireland

ISBN 1-879373-75-0
Library of Congress Catalog Card Number 94-65094

Printed in Hong Kong
Distributed in the United States and Canada
by Publishers Group West

8235
$//. 00

Early one winter morning, little Niko woke up to the sound of a tap.
He jumped out of bed and looked outside. The windowsill and all the

roofs were covered with snow. The ground was white and the sun looked like a great red ball against the grey sky. And there on the windowsill sat a little bird.

"Mother, look!"

"This is a chickadee," she said. "And it cannot find food because the snow has covered everything. So, let's make something for it to eat." Niko watched as she made a ball of plump seeds, chewy nuts and lard on a fir twig and put it into a window box on the balcony.

Niko saw the little chickadee come to the window box every day to peck at seeds and then fly away. As the weeks went by, the grey sky turned blue, the snow melted and the sun became warm and golden again. Then, one morning, the chickadee did not come to the window box for its food.

Niko was sad. He missed his friend.

"Where is the chickadee, mother?"

"Spring has come, Niko, and our friend can find food again," she said. "Let's throw away the dead twig and plant some flowers in the window box—red and white ones."

But, something was already growing in the window box! Niko spied two leaves on a stalk.

"Mother, look! Is this a flower, too?"

"Yes, Niko. This will grow into a sunflower. The chickadee dropped a seed and the warm sunshine has made it sprout."

"Will the flower be big?" Niko asked.

"Yes, very big indeed," his mother replied.

"Mother, will it be all grown tomorrow?"

"No, Niko, it will grow a little bit every day, all summer long." Niko thought that was a long time to wait. "Will the sunflower be grown when I'm as tall as daddy?" "No," mother said, "but if you water it, it will grow tall much faster. But, first, let's plant the sunflower in a big pot. It will need lots of room to grow."

So Niko and his mother put the sunflower in a new pot, and Niko said "I will water our new flower plant, and take good care of it."

The next day, Niko's dad brought a little watering can home. Spring turned into summer and Niko watered the sunflower every day. May turned to June and June to July. The sunflower grew bigger and bigger and made beautiful dark green leaves. Then one day, the sunflower was taller than Niko. When he looked up to the very tip top of the plant he saw a bud. And the bud got bigger and bigger and fatter and fatter.

August came and the days became very hot and sunny.
Then, one Saturday afternoon the bud opened up to be a
great sunflower. Niko was thrilled. "You are beautiful!
The bird brought you into the world. And,
you have drunk a lot of water! Once, you were as
small as my thumb. Now I must look up at you! You
are called Sunflower and your yellow petals are sunbeams around a brown circle with golden dots."

"Look, Niko," his mother said. "This is pollen. The
big black bumblebee is collecting it and now his legs
have yellow pants!" Niko was so happy.
The great bee liked the sunflower, too!

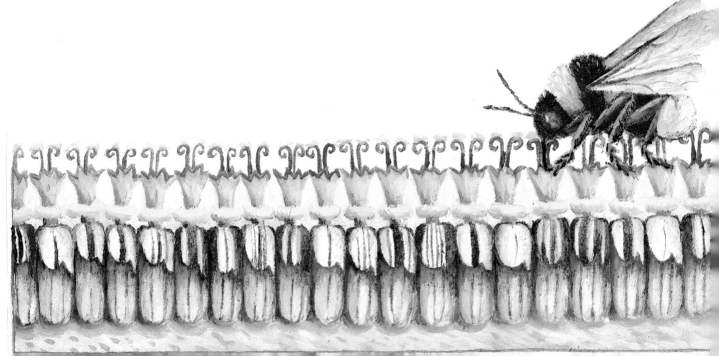

Then, August ended, and September began. The autumn sun wasn't as hot as the summer sun. So, the days became cooler as the seasons changed.

"Mother, look! The sunflower's yellow petals are falling to the ground. My flower is losing its sunbeams—is it sick?"

"No, Niko," his mother said. "The sunflower is all grown up, and its seeds are fat and ripe. See, it looks like a big plate filled with seeds. You can cut the flower and put it out next winter, after the snow falls. The birds will need food again. And our hungry little chickadee may return, to eat the food of the great flower that grew from the little seed that was left behind last spring."